Lions at the Library?

Zachary Williams

NEIGHBORHOOD READERS

Rosen Classroom Books & Materials™

New York

Lions are dancing at the library.
Can it be true?

Spaceships are landing at the library.
Can it be true?

Dinosaurs are singing at the library.
Can it be true?

Bears are eating at the library.
Can it be true?

Boats are sailing at the library.
Can it be true?

Flowers are growing at the library.
Can it be true?

A king and a queen are playing games
at the library.
Can it be true?

Snowmen are reading at the library.
Can it be true?

Camels are talking at the library.
Can it be true?

Do lions dance and dinosaurs sing
at the library?

Come to the library and read a book.
You will see!